For Rachel Claire
M.W.

For Genevieve
and Asher
B.F.

First published 1988 by Walker Books Ltd
87 Vauxhall Walk, London SE11 5HJ

This edition published 2005

2 4 6 8 10 9 7 5 3 1

Text © 1988 Martin Waddell
Illustrations © 1988 Barbara Firth

The right of Martin Waddell and Barbara Firth
to be identified as author and illustrator respectively
of this work has been asserted by them in accordance
with the Copyright, Designs and Patents Act 1988

This book has been typeset in Monotype Columbus

Printed in China

British Library Cataloguing in Publication Data:
a catalogue record for this book
is available from the British Library

ISBN 1-84428-109-4

www.walkerbooks.co.uk

WALKER BOOKS
AND SUBSIDIARIES
LONDON · BOSTON · SYDNEY · AUCKLAND

Can't You Sleep, Little Bear?

Martin Waddell

illustrated by Barbara Firth

Once there were two bears.
Big Bear and Little Bear.
Big Bear is the big bear, and Little Bear is the little bear.
They played all day in the bright sunlight. When night
came, and the sun went down, Big Bear took Little
Bear home to the Bear Cave.

Big Bear put Little Bear to bed
in the dark part of the cave.
"Go to sleep, Little Bear," he said.
And Little Bear tried.
Big Bear settled in the Bear Chair and
read his Bear Book, by the light of the fire.
But Little Bear couldn't get to sleep.

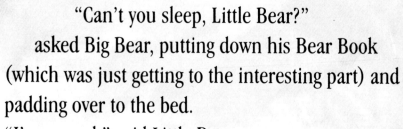

"Can't you sleep, Little Bear?"
asked Big Bear, putting down his Bear Book
(which was just getting to the interesting part) and
padding over to the bed.

"I'm scared," said Little Bear.

"Why are you scared, Little Bear?" asked Big Bear.

"I don't like the dark," said Little Bear.

"What dark?" said Big Bear.

"The dark all around us,"
said Little Bear.

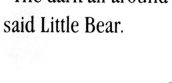

Big Bear looked, and he saw that the
dark part of the cave was very dark, so he went
to the Lantern Cupboard and took out the
tiniest lantern that was there.
Big Bear lit the tiniest lantern, and put it near
to Little Bear's bed.
"There's a tiny light to stop you being scared,
Little Bear," said Big Bear.
"Thank you, Big Bear," said Little Bear,
cuddling up in the glow.
"Now go to sleep, Little Bear," said Big Bear,
and he padded back to the Bear Chair and
settled down to read the Bear Book,
by the light of the fire.

Little Bear tried to
go to sleep, but he couldn't.
"Can't you sleep, Little Bear?" yawned Big Bear,
putting down his Bear Book (with just four pages to
go to the interesting bit) and padding over to the bed.
"I'm scared," said Little Bear.
"Why are you scared, Little Bear?" asked Big Bear.
"I don't like the dark," said Little Bear.
"What dark?" said Big Bear.
"The dark all around us," said Little Bear.
"But I brought you a lantern!" said Big Bear.
"Only a tiny-weeny one," said Little Bear. "And
there's lots of dark!"
Big Bear looked, and he saw that Little Bear was
quite right, there was still lots of dark. So Big Bear
went to the Lantern Cupboard and took out
a bigger lantern. Big Bear lit the lantern, and
put it beside the other one.

"Now go to sleep, Little Bear," said Big Bear
and he padded back to the Bear Chair and settled
down to read the Bear Book, by the light of the fire.
Little Bear tried and tried to go to sleep,
but he couldn't.

"Can't you sleep, Little Bear?" grunted Big Bear, putting down his Bear Book (with just three pages to go) and padding over to the bed.
"I'm scared," said Little Bear.
"Why are you scared, Little Bear?" asked Big Bear.
"I don't like the dark," said Little Bear.
"What dark?" asked Big Bear.
"The dark all around us," said Little Bear.
"But I brought you two lanterns!" said Big Bear.
"A tiny one and a bigger one!"
"Not much bigger," said Little Bear. "And there's still lots of dark."

Big Bear thought about it, and then
he went to the Lantern Cupboard
and took out the Biggest Lantern of
Them All, with two handles and a
bit of chain. He hooked the
lantern up above Little Bear's bed.
"I've brought you the Biggest Lantern
of Them All!" he told Little Bear.
"That's to stop you being scared!"
"Thank you, Big Bear," said Little
Bear, curling up in the glow and
watching the shadows dance.
"Now go to sleep, Little Bear," said Big
Bear and he padded back to the Bear
Chair and settled down to read the
Bear Book, by the light
of the fire.

Little Bear tried and tried and
tried to go to sleep,
but he couldn't.

"Can't you sleep, Little Bear?" groaned Big Bear,
putting down his Bear Book
(with just two pages to go)
    and padding over to the bed.

"I'm scared," said Little Bear.
"Why are you scared, Little Bear?" asked Big Bear.
"I don't like the dark," said Little Bear.
"What dark?" asked Big Bear.
"The dark all around us," said Little Bear.
"But I brought you the Biggest Lantern of Them All, and there isn't any dark left," said Big Bear.
"Yes, there is!" said Little Bear. "There is, out there!"
And he pointed out of the Bear Cave, at the night.

Big Bear saw that Little Bear was right.

Big Bear was very puzzled. All the lanterns in the world couldn't light up the dark outside. Big Bear thought about it for a long time, and then he said, "Come on, Little Bear."

"Where are we going?" asked Little Bear.

"Out!" said Big Bear.

"Out into the darkness?" said Little Bear.

"Yes!" said Big Bear.

"But I'm scared of the dark!" said Little Bear.

"No need to be!" said Big Bear, and he took Little Bear by the paw and led him out from the cave into the night

and it was…

DARK!

"Ooooh! I'm scared," said Little Bear,
cuddling up to Big Bear.
Big Bear lifted Little Bear, and
cuddled him, and said, "Look at the dark,
Little Bear." And Little Bear looked.

"I've brought you the moon, Little Bear," said Big Bear.
"The bright yellow moon, and all the twinkly stars."

But Little Bear didn't say anything, for he had gone
to sleep, warm and safe in Big Bear's arms.
Big Bear carried Little Bear back into the Bear Cave,
fast asleep, and he settled down with Little Bear
on one arm and the Bear Book on the other, cosy
in the Bear Chair by the fire.

And Big Bear read the Bear Book right to...

THE END

Close to the Heart

Close to the Heart

HELEN LOWRIE MARSHALL

Doubleday & Company, Inc.   Garden City, New York

1967

To
My Family

Contents

Close to the Heart

Close to the heart is a secret place
  Where dreams are stored away,
And sturdy candles of faith are kept
  Against the darker day.

And there, too, are the memories—
  The laughter shared, the tears,
The little things that mean so much,
  Seen through the mist of years.

Our dearest wishes, deepest loves,
  The burdens that we bear—
The essence of our being lies
  In what we harbor there.

To each his own—a hideaway
  That has no counterpart—
The treasure-house of the soul that lies
  Somewhere close to the heart.

—Where Dreams Are Stored Away

Who Dare to Dream

A few brave ones down through the years
Have dared to dream past others' fears;
Have dared to bridge the span between
The known and the unknown, unseen;
Have pushed on without hue or cry
In constant quest of 'how' and 'why';
Have probed the microscopic small;
Have faced the grim, forbidding wall
Of ignorance, disease and fear,
Acknowledging none as their peer;
Have led a timid world by hand
Into a strange, uncharted land.

Interpreters of God's great scheme
Are these—the brave who dare to dream.

Cadenza

The song of life is a dullish thing
   In its basic melody—
A cradle-to-grave, monotonous swing,
   Often in minor key.

But the Great Composer is very wise,
   For into every score
He adds cadenzas here and there
   That earth-bound hearts may soar—

Cadenzas of passion, vision, hope,
   And dreams—each plays a part.
Oh, the steady beat is for marching feet,
   But cadenzas—they're for the heart!

Window Shopping

I drive the quiet, lonely street,
Past homes with lights agleam,
And trials of the day seem to melt away
As I windowshop for a dream.

I glimpse the warmth and happiness
Bathed in their sea of light,
Pictures of home—the heart's desire,
Framed in the lonely night.

And my faith in the rightness of things returns,
In the fitness of God's great scheme,
And my heart remembers its song of hope
As I windowshop for a dream.

Anniversary

When first I dreamed of how our love would be,
So shallow was my dream, how could I see
The whole great, matchless depth of ripened love?
Can earthbound hearts envision Heaven above?

When first we two were sweethearts, you and I,
I did not dream how swift the time would fly;
How every perfect day would be, when gone,
The prelude to a still more perfect dawn.

In all my dreams I never knew the power
That love could have to sweeten every hour;
The quiet joy I find in your caress,
The sweet content of our togetherness.

The dream was just a glimpse God gave to me,
One fleeting glimpse of sweet reality.

The Real You

Don't be afraid to see yourself
  As the you-that-you'd-like-to-be,
No matter how far removed from the real
  The you-of-your-dreams may be.

Keep dreaming the dream—hitch a ride on a star,
  Hold tight—never let yourself fall,
And one day you'll find that the you-of-your-dreams
  Is the you-that-is-real, after all.

Who See Beyond

They scoff—let us have no more dreams, they say,
'Tis Truth, not dreams, we have need of today—
Stark Truth, that sees things as they really are,
Not childish wishing on some distant star,
Nor visionary fantasy of peace—
Give us the Truth—and let this dreaming cease!

But dreamers have a way of dreaming on,
And beauty's still a part of every dawn.
And, though the realists say Truth is dark
And must, like winter's trees, be bare and stark—
The dreamer visions leaves on barren bough—
Ah, but the world needs dreamers like these now.

Dreamers, who see the promises that lie
Behind the sodden grayness of the sky—
Dreamers who weave their shining silver web
Of faith, that holds when hope and courage ebb;
Who look beyond the present fear and doubt
And see the sun when shadow's all about.

You, then, who would be real, scoff not the dream,
Though gossamer and fragile it may seem;
Scorn not its strength, for when all's said and done,
You'll find that Truth, itself, and Dreams are one.

Five, Ten, Fifteen, Twenty

At five, her dream was rather sweet—
She would marry the little boy up the street.
(He did have a most engaging grin
That showed where his two front teeth had been.)
She would live in a house by an apple tree
And raise an enormous family!

At ten, her dreams took quite a flair—
She would marry a handsome millionaire
Who'd cheerfully grant her all her wishes.
She would have a maid to do the dishes
And she would be a famous star,
Complete with pool and foreign car!

At fifteen, her dream's central feature?
Why, naturally, her history teacher—
Balding and married and thirty-five,
And barely aware that she was alive.
A spinster she would always be,
True to her love eternally!

At twenty—what's this, a repeat?
Back to the same boy up the street.
(He still has the same engaging grin,
But now his two front teeth are in.)
She dreams of a house with an apple tree.
And of, some day, raising a family.

Try a Dream On

Sometime when you're feeling a trifle blue,
And the clouds hang grey in your skies,
Take a shopping trip into Make-Believe—
Try a Dream on—just for size.

Take plenty of time to shop around,
Look them over, and pick and choose.
After all, you don't have to buy the Dream,
So what do you have to lose?

And do pass up the sensible ones.
Pick out something jolly, instead—
The gayest, most frivolous Dream you can find—
Then swirl it over your head.

Let it fall into place till its glittering folds
Enwrap you from head to toe,
And you'll find yourself dancing away on a star,
The very first thing you know!

It might even be that the Dream you try
Will fit so well that you'll buy it;
But you'll never know till you let yourself go—
Next time you're blue, won't you try it?

Gone With the Dawn

My dreams are all such intangible things,
They wander the night on their frivolous wings;
But just let me waken and try to recall—
A few disconnected fragments is all
That's left—plus a feeling of blank frustration,
As though I'd been left in a mad situation,
A silly and wholly illogical trend
Without a beginning, or middle, or end.

I envy the fellow who always is able
To relive his dream at the breakfast table,
With not one illogical sequence about it.
I envy his mem'ry—but frankly, I doubt it!

Spring Heart Cleaning

I cleaned my heart out yesterday.
I steeled myself to throw away
Quite all the precious, foolish hoard
Of memories and dreams I'd stored.

Courageously, I cleared each room
And swept it clean with Reason's broom,
Till every little nook was bare
And not a single memory there.

No dream—no musty might-have-been—
And then I saw—
You'd crept back in.

Never Again

My heart was a garden, prim and trim,
Orderly, row on row—
Each emotion in place,
Each memory its space,
And everything just so.

Then I met you—and a strange breeze blew
And my garden lay tense in its waiting.
As the shadows lengthened
The strange breeze strengthened
With never a sign of abating—

Till you kissed me, and then, oh, never again
Will my heart be a model of neatness.
Since that wonderful day
When Love swept it away,
It's a shamble—a shamble of sweetness!

— Candles of Faith

Morning Prayer

Good morning, Lord,
  Another lovely day—
Help me to keep it so,
  Dear Lord, I pray.

May no small, careless word
  Or deed of mine
Let fall a shadow there
  To spoil the shine;

No act of kindness,
  Thoughtlessly undone,
Make dim this lovely morning's
  Bright, clean sun.

Help me to keep this day
  As good as new,
Till at its close I give
  It back to you.

Each day, upon my daily round,
I find myself on holy ground—
The morning-glories on my fence
Inspire quiet reverence.
Just one small, tender seedling grew,
And now, this miracle in blue.
A robin in the apple tree
Sings out his glad doxology.
I hear the pure, unsullied joy
Of laughter from a little boy;
I bow before the firm belief
And faith of one who lives with grief;
I watch a jet plane skim the skies
And marvel at man's enterprise;
I look upon a field of wheat
And thank God for the bread we eat;
I watch the benedictive rain
On low-bowed heads of flower and grain.
A friend drops in, a neighbor calls,
The lamps are lit, night gently falls;
Contentment settles with the sun
In labors of the day well done.
So many little altars there,
So many simple calls to prayer,
So many reasons for thanksgiving—
The sacraments of daily living.

The Little and the Near

Would you birth a better day?
Then be content to start
In little ways, and near ways,
And ways of simple art;

With little things and near things
And things of everyday,
For big things and better things
Are born in just this way.

Big things and better things
And things of great moment,
Are first a dream and then a scheme,
And then long hours spent

In quiet ways and patient ways
And ways of faith and love.
This is the pattern and the law
Of Him who reigns above.

He, too, foresaw a better day,
A world of peace and joy,
But He began in simple way
With one small baby Boy.

I Give You These—

To those who bear a cross—I give you these—

The picture of a garden, and of One
    kneeling in prayer, alone, at set of sun;
    alone, as only you can understand—
    a stranger in a once familiar land.

The echo of His agonizing prayer
    that, floating still upon the troubled air,
    unites all heavy hearts in sympathy—
    in common with the Man of Galilee.

The story of that first glad Easter day—
    the tidings that the stone was rolled away,
    The hope that's wafted on the springtime breeze—

    To those who bear a cross—
            I give you these.

Living Prayer

Prayer has many forms, I think.
In ways, far more than words, we link
Our hearts and souls to God. Perhaps
By just simple deed man taps
That Reservoir of Strength. No need
For words—his prayer lies in his deed.

Contrition, adoration, love,
Devotion to his God above—
All praise, all glory, all thanksgiving,
Are manifest in daily living.
Words are as empty as the air
Unless we truly live our prayer.

Christmas Love Story

A simple little man he was,
His clothing worn and poor,
Doing his Christmas shopping
In a crowded ten cent store.

A shiny, new tin pan, three dishcloths,
Chosen with such care,
You knew that he had never owned
A penny he could spare.

A brave, gay paper lamp shade,
A yard of oilcloth, neat;
A wistful look at price tags
His few cents could not meet.

And then, on weary feet he turned
Where glittering nosegays lay,
And with his last few pennies
Bought a holiday bouquet.

"It's for my wife for Christmas—
She likes pretty things," he said.
I blinked—and could have sworn
I saw a halo 'round his head.

True Measure

How long we live is not for us to say;
We may have years ahead—or but a day.
The length of life is not of our control,
But length is not the measure of the soul—
Not length, but width and depth define the span
By which the world takes measure of a man.
It matters not how long before we sleep,
But only how wide is our life—how deep.

Youth's Prayer

Dear Lord—You, who were once as young as we,
Help us to be the persons we should be.
You know the dreams we dream, the hopes we hold,
The secret longings we have never told.

You know, too, how temptations cross our way,
Help us, dear Lord, to meet them day by day,
Strong in the knowledge You are on our side.
Help us to conquer selfish, thoughtless pride.

Help us to grow as You grew here on earth,
In wisdom, and in stature, and in worth;
And, in that growing, let us ever lend
A helping hand to those who need a friend.

Give us a goal that we may ever strive—
For in that striving we shall keep alive.
Help us to live for right and truth and Thee—
Help us to be the persons we should be.

Grateful

I'm grateful for the privilege of prayer,
Grateful I can call and know He's there;
Grateful for the peace that floods my soul,
For the strength to press on toward the goal,
For the faith that banishes all doubt,
For the hope that puts my fears to route;
Grateful for the sweet surcease from care—
Grateful for the privilege of prayer.

Afterglow

I'd like the memory of me
To be a happy one.
I'd like to leave an afterglow
Of smiles when day is done.

I'd like to leave an echo
Whispering softly down the ways,
Of happy times, and laughing times
And bright and sunny days.

I'd like the tears of those who grieve
To dry before the sun
Of happy memories I leave
Behind—when day is done.

Prayer at the New Year

At this, the time of high-borne resolutions,
I, too, would offer up this earnest prayer—
That I may know the priceless worth of friendships,
And keep those friendships always in repair;

That I may never take a love for granted,
Or lightly treat the thoughts of those who care,
But treasure every friendship's precious cargo—
And keep those friendships always in repair.

When Wonder Dies

When wonder dies within man's eyes,
   Then man, indeed, is old.
When man can look upon the skies,
   Its mysteries untold,
And in his heart and soul feel not
   A sense of wonder there,
Nor ponder o'er a freshing breeze
   Or on a blossom fair,
Or watch the person of a child
   Through years of growth unfold—
When wonder dies within man's eyes,
   Then man, indeed, is old.

32

The Miracle of

I, Myself, am my own
Of miracles today.
My body molded as all
Yet more than human
I am Myself—my min
My store of memory.
I am the keeper of
I, only, hold the ke
And, such a soul as
Of great or little v
Has not been dup
By another soul
I am Myself, dis
Yet part of one
The miracle ma
A self, the hun

—The Laughter Shared, the Tears

Going on Fifteen

We have a stranger in the house these days,
  A stranger with the most amazing ways!

He came one day, to both my grief and joy,
  The day I lost, somewhere, my *little* boy.

I never cease to marvel at him there—
  The length of him upon my small son's chair!

The overwhelming bigness of his feet,
  His clumsy, tender ways, so new, so sweet.

The way his hair stays combed! This much I know,
  My *little* son's wild mop was never so!

And when he speaks—stark wonder strikes my face.
  Wherever did he get that booming bass!

In all his dignity of fourteen years
  I dare not ask him if he's washed his ears,

And so I take a furtive look, unseen,
  And find them both amazing pink and clean!

And, deep inside, it hurts a little so—
  The kind of hurt that only mothers know.

That dear, but dirty, little boy I had—
  He surely cannot be this spotless lad.

I watch his newfound charm beguile the girls,
  Remembering how he used to pull their curls;

I see him trying men's clothes on for size,
  And, somehow, there's a mist before my eyes.

But then I find my rifled cookie jar
  And know my *little* boy is not gone far.

High Chair Champ

This is real courage that we see here,
So make with the praise and get ready to cheer.

No smallish feat this—why, just *see* how far!
(Depending, of course, on how little you are.)

Watch how he pauses there at the brink.
What are his feelings now? What does he think?

Is he afraid, this courageous one?
Will he retreat? Will he turn now and run?

No—there, off he jumps! And lands on all four,
All the way
            from the bottom-most step
                        to the floor!

Cheers for the champion! Bring forth the cup!
With the very best milk in the house fill it up!

He's dauntless, he's daring,
  He's brave, and he's bold,
      He's dear, and he's dirty,
          And he's two years old!

The Miracle

Now, two little frogs in the course of their way,
Fell into a pitcher of cream one day,
And though they both frantically struggled about,
Quite obviously, neither one could get out.

Whereupon, said the first, "Why struggle at all?
The cream is too deep and the pitcher too tall.
I could have leaped out if I had had room."
Thus, blaming his fate, he sank down to his doom.

But the second frog said, "Now, I must confess,
I've certainly got myself into a mess.
Things look mighty bad, but at least, I can fight,"
And he began kicking with all of his might;
And he thrashed and he struggled; he splashed and
  he tore,
And when he grew weary, he only thrashed more,
Till a miracle happened, as miracles do
For the fellow who just won't admit that he's
  through—
The cream he was kicking grew thicker and thick
Until there was finally no more need to kick!

And, wondering how such good luck came about,
He crouched on the butter he'd made—and leaped
  out!

Hurrah for Thanksgiving Day!

Over the river and through the woods
  To Grandmother's house we go—
The traffic is awful and Daddy is mad
  'Cause he has to drive so slow.

Mommy is nervous—she says, "Now, Dad,
  Please do drive carefully!"
Then Daddy gets madder and says, "Now, look,
  I'm doing the driving—See!"

Us kids get to fighting—I don't know why,
  And I get a sock in the nose.
And Mommy says, "Shame on you—look at you now,
  You've ruined your Thanksgiving clothes!"

The baby wakes up and begins to cry,
  He's hungry and cold and wet.
Seems like we've been driving for ever and ever
  And we're not to Grandma's house yet.

But finally we make it—oh, wonderful day,
  Oh, day of thanksgiving and cheer!
Mom gives Dad a look as we start to unload
  And says, "Well, at least, we got here!"

Grandma is waiting with door swung wide,
  "Come in," she calls, "Come in!"
But you can hardly hear her voice
  For all the noise and din.

"The first touch-down for Notre Dame,"
  She yells above the clatter.
"Happy Thanksgiving—we're late," Mom yells.
  Gram says, "It doesn't matter."

"Just grab a snack and come in here
  Where everyone can see."
And Dad says, "Now, you kids pipe down,
  We want to watch TV."

So—we eat cold turkey and watch the game
  And when it's finally done
Dad says we'd better be starting home.
  He's mad cause Navy won.

So, back through the woods and across the bridge
  Once more we're on our way.
Hurrah for cold turkey, hurrah for TV,
  Hurrah for Thanksgiving Day!

They'll Never Know

Children, now-days, have a lot
That we kids never had,
And, probably, they think
The 'good old days' were pretty bad;
But there's one joy they'll never know
And none can quite compare
With that day when Ma let us shed
Our winter underwear!

Yes, sir, in those days Spring
Was something to look forward to.
We kids would beg for weeks,
But Ma would say, "No, it won't do;
You'll catch your death of cold,
There's still a chillness in the air.
When it gets good and warm,
Then you can shed your underwear."

And when we'd just about decided
Spring would never come,
There'd be the day when Ma would say
To take it off, by gum!
Then—talk about your freedom!
Why, no butterfly in June
Ever felt more light and airy
Crawling out of his cocoon!

No more bulges in your stockings,
No more scratchin' round your neck,
No more sweatin', no more bindin'—
You were free once more, by heck!
Yes, sir, kids today are lucky,
With their legs and arms all bare,
But they'll never know what bliss it is
To shed long underwear!

Mother-Talk

Mary—was that little Boy of yours
   Ever naughty at all?
Did He always do what you wanted Him to?
   Did He always come at your call?
Or did He cry when you scrubbed his ears
   And bolt at the sight of a comb?
Did He ever "show off" and embarrass you
   When you had guests in your home?

And did He balk at going to bed
   And delay it as long as He could?
Was there ever a time when your little Boy
   Was *anything* but good?
But, after a specially trying day
   When you'd finally tucked Him in,
Did you find your love crowding out all thought
   Of the naughty boy He'd been?

And did you tiptoe in to see,
   And did you breathe a prayer
For help in guiding that little Boy
   Sleeping so sweetly there?
Oh, Mary, you had a little Son,
   You know what I'm trying to say—
My own little boy that I love so dear—
   I had to spank him today!

So Little

There is so little I can do
  To ease your hour of pain,
So very little I can do
  To bring the sun again.

I seem to find no words to tell
  How very much I care;
The phrases fall so clumsily
  Upon the grief-filled air.

And so I bake a pie—a cake—
  A loaf of homemade bread,
And hope that they will say the words
  My lips have left unsaid;

That through them you will know my heart
  Is reaching out to you—
There is so little I can say,
  So little I can do.

Grandmothers

They say that all grandmothers
    Are inclined to brag a bit,
And that there is some truth in this
    I frankly must admit;

For, since I've reached the Grandma stage,
    And all my friends have, too,
I'm simply floored by all the bragging
    These grandmothers do.

To hear them rave, you'd think for sure
    That this old human race
Was fast becoming supermen
    At a tremendous pace!

Yet, when I see these boys and girls—
    Their Grandma's pride and joy—
Each one seems to be quite an ordinary
    Girl or boy!

Of course, I humor them along
    And say I think they're fine—
But you can see the difference
    If you've ever noticed mine!

Man

n is a very peculiar creature.
ps the most outstanding feature
marks his hopelessly masculine mind
inability to find
ng. He'll simply swear
nkety-blankety thing isn't there!
whatever-it-is is right in place,
to see as the nose on your face,
less routine will never vary—
l for his wife or his secretary.
their efficiency put him to shame?
dly! He acts as though they were to blame!
line dignity suffers no loss;
the lord of creation, the boss!
may grumble, complain and deride,
ey've a certain nice feeling inside—
f power, importance, content,
things were going the way they were

ce Eve, man's opposite sex
lly broken their beautiful necks
him as though he were a king.
e poor soul can't find anything!
that way—he's our pride and our joy—
he's still just a big little boy!

My own are so much cuter, smarter,
  Handsomer than theirs,
I can afford to humor them
  When they put on such airs!

I'm really glad that I don't brag
  Like other Grandmas do—
I've so much more to brag about
  If I just wanted to!

Too Many Irons

One's time should be pleasantly occupied,
  The wise psychologists state.
The lady of leisure with time on her hands
  Is definitely out of date.
So—keeping in tune with the trend of the times—
  The versatile life we admire—
I graciously joined this and that, here and there,
  Putting iron upon iron in the fire.

And now—am I pleasantly occupied?
  Would you honestly like to know?
I'm not only pleasantly occupied—
  I'm madly, hysterically so!

48

To My Cal

(Who Is an Immaculat

You make me see the wor
The children's finger-print
The dust accumulated on
The spot not vacuumed

Your prim perfection b
But still, I guess you'r
You always make me
The minute that you

Hallowe'en Treat

This is the night my lonely door
Shall open to a score or more
Of friends. I've baked from early dawn—
Tonight my cakes will all be gone.
The doughnuts and the cider, too,
Will disappear like witch's brew
To chubby ghosts with grubby hands,
To visitors from foreign lands;
To Chinamen with stocking queues,
Spanish girls in Mother's shoes,
Pirates bold, patch over eye,
Tiny cowboys, stranger-shy,
A wicked witch with cardboard hat,
Funny clowns all pillow-fat,
Skeletons with painted bones—
With shrieks and laughter, groans and moans,
They'll ring my too long silent bell
And troop inside. I'll treat them well;
And when my goodies all are gone,
Their painted circus will move on;
But every dressed-up girl and boy
Will bring my old heart warmth and joy,
Although I know, till next year's treat,
I'll be just the 'old lady up the street.'

Where Do Little Sneezes Go?

There's a question that's pressing,
In fact, quite distressing—
I've wondered since I was a child.
You feel a sneeze coming,
Your nostrils start strumming,
The itching is driving you wild!

By all intuition
It should reach fruition,
But Emily Post says, "Thumbs down!"
You must throttle it, bottle it,
Surely not coddle it
Or risk Society's frown!

So, yearning to pop it,
You manfully stop it.
Assuming a nonchalant pose,
You curb its wild passion
In time-honored fashion
With finger pressed under your nose.

Till, finally, elated,
Though somewhat deflated,
You breathe once again with some ease—
But still I'm left guessing,
The question still pressing—
Whatever becomes of the sneeze?

—Through the Mist of Years

The Old Base-Burner

Remember how, come Fall, we'd haul
  The old base-burner in
From where Ma had it stored each Spring
  Out in the old feed bin?

Recall that special, pungent smell
  The fresh new stove-black made,
And all the warm excitement when
  The first Fall fire was laid?

Remember how we used to fight
  To get that favorite spot
Behind the stove, so we could dress
  Where it was nice and hot?

And that all-too-short moment
  Of solid blissfulness
To stand there naked, warm and free
  Before Ma made us dress?

That moment when your skin drank in
  The old stove's good warm air
Before you had to case it up
  In that long underwear.

Remember how the wraps hung near,
  The overshoes below—
How snug and warm they always felt
  When it was time to go?

And then, how good to come back home
  When it was cold and snowing
And see the old base-burner with
  Its isinglass a-glowing.

And put our mittens 'round the top
  To dry, stiff, warm and cozy,
And sit around and toast our toes
  Till everyone got dozey.

Of course, the modern furnace
  Beats the old a thousand ways,
But something fine went out, I think,
  With those base-burner days.

Perspective

Long ago when we were smaller,
Grownups then were much, much taller,
Men were stronger, braver, bolder,
Old was ever so much older!

Skies were wider and much bluer,
Grass was greener, clouds were fewer,
Nights were darker, stars were brighter,
Snows far deeper and much whiter.

Food was yummier, odors headier,
Fun was easier, laughter readier,
Life much simpler, all in all,
In those days when we were small.

How Is a Mother Remembered?

How is a mother remembered?
Hands busy sewing buttons,
Or dishing up good-smelling things
For hungry little gluttons;

Voice softly humming as she worked
About the house or garden;
The goodnight kiss when you'd been bad
That brought such peace and pardon;

The heavenly smell of homemade bread,
Its warm, moist, special goodness;
The disapproving look when you
Were guilty of some rudeness.

A row of plants upon the sill,
With such care watched and tended;
And stacks of underwear and sox
All neatly darned and mended;

The bedtime stories, and the fun
Of teasing for another—
So many little things make up
The memory of Mother.

My Home Town

I grew up
Like a carefree pup
In a little midwest town;
And those small-town days
With their small-town ways
Seem worthy of some renown.

There was the band
In the old bandstand—
The music was plenty poor;
But we played real loud,
And the town was proud,
And that's really what bands are for.

There was basketball
In the old Town Hall.
We played a terrible game.
But, though our score
Was always poor,
They cheered us just the same.

There was Sunday School.
As a general rule,
Most everybody went.
Our attention strayed
When the preacher prayed,
But, at least, it made a dent.

There were special days,
Programs and plays—
Didn't set the world agog;
But that small-town school
Was our own little pool
Where each was a great big frog!

Every talent we had,
Good, medium, bad,
Was given a chance to show;
And who can say
That our life today
From some such seed didn't grow?

I sometimes pity
The kids in the city,
Though they'd be the first to frown
On the simple joys
Of the girls and boys
Who grew up in a little town.

Crazy Quilt

Whenever we're sick at our house,
   Me, or Mugsie, or Milt
Mom feels of our head then says "Oh-oh,
   It's you for the crazy quilt!"
Then she gets it down out of the cupboard
   And spreads it out over the bed,
And then we don't mind being sick near so much
   Or having a tempachure head.

'Cause we have a game we made up ourselves,
   To play with the crazy quilt,
And nobody knows it 'cept Granny and Mom
   And me and Mugsie and Milt.
Whoever is sick gets to choose the patch,
   Green or yellow or pink,
And Granny's the teller, with Mom to help
   Sometimes, when Granny can't think.

Like, maybe, we'll pick a blue patch,
   And Granny will say, "My land,
That's a piece of the shirt your Grandpa wore
   When he used to play in the band.
He'd march along with the big bass drum
   And oh how the old town rang!
Nobody could ever play like Gramps
   With such a boomity-bang!"

Or, maybe, we'll choose the yellow one
    With the flowers all spraggled there,
Then Granny will say, "Why, that's the dress
    I wore to the County Fair.
That was the day I met your Gramps,
    And my cherry pie won the prize."
Then Granny will get all dreamy-like
    With a faraway look in her eyes.

There's one I like that's a red one.
    It's a piece of a bright red shirt,
A fireman's shirt, and it used to belong
    To my favorite Uncle Bert.
I can see him clangin' that old bell,
    And zoomin' away to a fire,
And I get so excited, sometimes, Mom says
    It makes my tempachure higher!

We don't mind being sick at our house,
    Me, nor Mugsie, nor Milt,
'Cause there's more keen stories than you ever heard
    Sewed up in that crazy quilt!

Jelly Makin' Time

It's jelly-makin' time again,
The grapes are thick as hops.
Pa's s'posed to be out pickin',
But now and then he stops
To argue politics with
Old Man Mosley 'cross the way.
Can't blame him much for loafin',
It's a loafin' sort of day—

That lazy, hazy kind of weather
Like it's mournin' so
To think how soon the flowers
Will be covered up with snow.
Old Rover's out there tearin' 'round
As frisky as a pup;
He sure does love them dry leaves;
Shame we have to rake 'em up.

Jes' see that mornin' glory—
Might' near covers that whole wall;
And those sunflowers Pa likes so—
They must be ten foot tall.
But, land sakes, here I stand
A-ruminatin' in the sun
And all them pans of grapes in there
A-waitin' to be done!

Grandma's House

When I was three, till I was seven
I lived just down the road from Heaven.

You might not think that it was much—
An old brown house, a yard and such.

The 'pearly gate' had a hinge that squeaked,
The 'mansion fair' a roof that leaked;

But there was an angel living there,
An angel with soft greying hair,

Whose cooky jar was always handy,
Just like her stock of peppermint candy.

No matter how bad I had been,
What childish mischief I'd been in,

I found a special sort of grace
Reserved for me at Grandma's place.

Oh yes, she spoiled me, that I know,
But, oh, we both enjoyed it so!

We had our own small bit of Heaven
When I was three, till I was seven.

Responsive Chords

How many times has someone said
    Some simple, trivial thing
That seemed to strike your own heartstrings
    And make them start to sing?

Responsive chords that harmonize
    In some mysterious way
With something you've experienced
    Perhaps, some bygone day.

Responsive chords that for a while
    Bring back a smile, a tear,
The melody that memory makes
    Of things we once held dear.

And if I shall have struck that chord—
    If some word I have said
Has set your heartstrings singing,
    Then, indeed, am I well paid.